For Mark and Annemarie,
who love elephants (and cheese)! ~ T. W.

tiger tales
5 River Road, Suite 128, Wilton, CT 06897
Published in the United States 2015
Originally published in Great Britain 2015
by Little Tiger Press
Text and illustrations copyright © 2015 Tim Warnes
Visit Tim Warnes at www.ChapmanandWarnes.com
ISBN-13: 978-1-58925-174-8
ISBN-10: 1-58925-174-1
Printed in China
LTP/1400/0994/0914

For more insight and activities,
visit us at www.tigertalesbooks.com

Disguises

# The Great Cheese Robbery

by Tim Warnes

tiger tales

Daddy Elephant was as big and strong as a tractor.

Patrick was small and only a little bit strong.

Patrick was scared of a lot of things, like the dark, ghosts, bees, and the fluff you find under the sofa.

Daddy wasn't scared of anything.

Patrick tried and tried to scare Daddy Elephant, but it never worked.

"It's not fair," sighed Patrick.
"You're not scared of anything!"

But there was **ONE** thing that
Daddy Elephant was afraid of . . . .

One afternoon, there was a squeak at the door.

"Look, Daddy," gasped Patrick. "A teeny-tiny elephant!"

"That's not an elephant!" cried Daddy.

IT'S A M-M-M-MOUSE!

"Good day, gentlemen," said the mouse. "My name is Cornelius J. Parker, from the Cheese Inspection Council. I'm here to inspect your cheese."

"W-w-we don't have any," stammered Daddy Elephant.

"Yes, we do," said Patrick helpfully, "in the refrigerator. I'll show you."

Cornelius J. Parker made a very thorough inspection indeed.

Cornelius opened his briefcase and pulled out a walkie-talkie.

Soon there was another squeak
at the door.

"We're here for the refrigerator,"
said a mouse.

"The refrigerator?" asked Patrick.

"We're confiscating it on grounds
of health and safety," said the other
mouse.

"B-b-but I'm making macaroni and cheese tonight," said Daddy.

"It's his signature dish," Patrick added.

"Not anymore, it's not!" said Cornelius.

Mascarpone!
Manchego!
Follow me!

There was an awful

SGREEK!

as the mice slid and scraped the refrigerator across the floor.

Then the refrigerator fell with a mighty

CRASH!

"Don't worry—I'll help!" called Patrick.

Suddenly, there was a loud cry from the living room.

and not just the refrigerator. The mice took the T. V., the phone, the fish, the cookies, the lamp . . .

even Patrick's toys!

Daddy Elephant gave a little whimper as the mice cheered and lifted up the sofa.

STOP! THAT'S MY DADDY!

Patrick shouted in his biggest, strongest voice. But the mice ignored him.

Just then . . .

"Put my husband down OR ELSE!"
shouted Mommy Elephant.

# Everyone froze.

Cornelius narrowed his eyes.
"Or else, what?"
Patrick's Mommy took a big,
deep breath and . . .

"The truth is, Patrick," said Mommy Elephant, "everyone's afraid of something—even your big old dad!"

"But he's still the biggest, strongest elephant around," said Patrick.

"I am," smiled Daddy proudly. "But when it comes to mice . . .

## Mommy's the bravest!"